Malorie BLACKMAN

With illustrations by Paul Fisher-Johnson

Barrington Stoke

www.malorieblackman.co.uk

First published in 2015 in Great Britain by
Barrington Stoke Ltd
18 Walker Street, Edinburgh, EH3 7LP

www.barringtonstoke.co.uk

This story was first published in a different form in
Out of this World (Orion, 1997)

Text © 1997 Oneta Malorie Blackman
Illustrations © 2015 Paul Fisher-Johnson

The moral right of Oneta Malorie Blackman and
Paul Fisher-Johnson to be identified as the author and illustrator
of this work has been asserted in accordance with the Copyright,
Designs and Patents Act, 1988

A CIP catalogue record for this book is available
from the British Library upon request

ISBN: 978-1-78112-460-4

Printed in China by Leo

For Neil and Lizzy, with love as always

CONTENTS

CHAPTER 1
FIVE-A-SIDE

Beep! Beep! Beep!

Someone wanted to talk to Cal.

"Answer call," Cal said. He wondered if he'd ever finish his homework.

The map of Neptune's blue-green clouds that he'd been studying vanished in a flash and his best friend Jenna's face appeared instead.

"Cal, I've got some bad news," Jenna said. For once she wasn't smiling.

"Hello to you too!" Cal said. "What's the matter?"

"It's about our football match tomorrow."

"What about it?" Cal asked. He was on high alert.

"Jacob's been asking questions," Jenna said. Her face was grim.

"Oh no!" Cal's heart sank.

Jenna shook her head, and her lips screwed up with fury.

Jacob was Jenna's twin brother and Cal knew that Jenna hated him even more than Cal or any of their other friends did. Jacob never thought of anyone but himself. He set a new standard for being totally and utterly selfish.

"I told him that it's a five-a-side game and we already have ten players, but he says we have to let him sit in as a reserve."

"And what did you say?" Cal asked.

"I told him that he couldn't, of course," Jenna said. "But you know what Jacob's like. That won't stop him. So I thought I'd better call everyone before the game to warn them."

Cal was angry now. "How did Jacob find out about the game in the first place?" he demanded.

"Hey! Don't bite my head off," Jenna snapped back. "I didn't tell him."

Cal took a deep breath, then another, in an effort to calm down.

Jacob knew about their game ...

It was dangerous enough to play football the way they played it. Now that Jacob had found out about it, they'd have to worry about him as well.

"What's Jacob doing now?" Cal asked.

"He's calling everyone to try to find out who else is playing," Jenna said. "He's hoping that someone will say it's OK for him to sit in as the reserve."

"Did he ask where we were playing?" Cal asked.

"Yeah, but I told him not to be so nosy," Jenna said. "I said if he wasn't playing then he didn't need to know."

"That won't stop him," Cal said.

"I know." Jenna sighed.

Cal clenched his fists inside his Non-Contact suit. How on earth had Jacob found out about their football match? It didn't make sense. None of the team would have told him – Cal was sure of that. They all had too much to lose if anyone outside the team found out what was going on.

Jenna turned away from her screen to listen to something Cal couldn't hear. "I've got to go," she said, as she turned back to face him. "Dad's calling me. See you tomorrow."

"Maybe we should cancel tomorrow's match – just to be on the safe side?" Cal said.

"No way! You can't do that," Jenna said. "We only get to play once a month as it is. I've been looking forward to our game since the day after the last one!"

"It's better to postpone the game tomorrow than risk being found out," Cal said.

"That would be much worse – we'd never get to play again."

Jenna pursed her lips. "I suppose so," she agreed. "Look, call me tomorrow morning and let me know what's happening."

"Disconnect call," Cal said.

Jenna's face vanished.

CHAPTER 2
CAUTION

After the call to Jenna disconnected, the green-blue clouds of Neptune moved across the screen again. Cal tried to focus, but he wasn't in the mood for homework. His mind was buzzing.

Cal's mum popped her head around his bedroom door.

"Hey, Cal," she said. "Your dinner's ready."

"Mum ..." Cal swivelled around in his chair. "Mum, what would happen if I took off my NC suit?"

"Take off your Non-Contact suit?" Cal's mum was horrified. She came into the room. "It's forbidden – and it's dangerous," she said. "You wouldn't ever do it, would you?"

"No." Cal shook his head. "I just wondered what would happen if I did?"

"You'd die," Cal's mum said. "Without our NC suits, we'd all die. They protect us from pollution and fall-out and disease."

"Yes, but …"

"No 'buts'." His mum shook her head. "I'm not messing about, Cal. Direct contact with another person would be lethal."

Cal turned back to his computer.

"Oh, Cal," his mum said. Her voice was a bit softer now. "Don't you think I'd love to give you a hug – a proper hug – without our NC suits between us? Don't you think I'd love to hold my own son? But it's too dangerous. We humans almost got wiped off the planet when I was a little girl, because of the diseases spread by the contact we had with other people. Believe me, this way is much safer."

"I guess so," Cal said. "I just wonder sometimes what it would be like to touch someone's arm. Or to know what other people smell like. Or to see someone smile without an NC mask over their face."

Mum frowned. "What's brought this on all of a sudden?"

"Nothing in particular," Cal replied. He was on dangerous ground now. He shouldn't have said anything. Mum was no fool and she'd suspect something if Cal kept asking more questions.

"Sorry, Mum," Cal said. "I'll have my dinner now."

Cal walked over to the meal unit in his room and slotted in the feed tube of his NC suit.

He watched as his dinner was pumped along the tube and directly into his stomach. The tube in his stomach would only work with an official feed tube, so it was 100% safe and it sealed shut when it wasn't in use.

Cal wondered again what it would be like to chew and taste real, solid food. It was weird to think of chewing your food, but Cal knew that's what people had to do long ago. So many things had changed ... Cal's thoughts turned back to the football match.

'What was Jacob playing at?' he thought. Cal knew he'd be trying to find out more about the game, no doubt.

And what if he did find out ...?

Cal shook his head. They'd all just have to make sure that he didn't. There'd be hell to pay otherwise.

Cal frowned. Something wasn't right. With a start, he turned his head to see his mum watching him. The silence between them crackled. Neither of them said a word.

"Cal, be careful – OK?" his mum said at last.

Before Cal could answer, she left the room.

CHAPTER 3
TACKLE

Jacob called the next morning, while Cal and his family were plugged into the meal unit for their breakfast.

Cal went into his bedroom to take the call, which made his mum and dad smile. He guessed what Jacob was calling about – and he wasn't wrong.

"Hi, Cal." Jacob's smile was bright and false on the screen. "How are you?"

"Fine."

"I ... er ... I hear you and Jenna and some others are playing football this afternoon," Jacob said.

"So?" Cal said. He was pleased to see that Jacob's smile slipped a little at the short answer.

"Jenna said to ask you," Jacob said. "Can I play too?"

"No," Cal said, his voice crisp. "It's five-a-side. We have everyone we need." He was annoyed at Jenna for passing the buck to him.

"But I could be reserve in case someone can't make it or has to leave the game before it's over," Jacob pleaded. "Please ..."

"No."

"At least tell me where you're playing so I can set up my screen at home to watch," said Jacob.

"No. It's a private game."

"Oh, come on," Jacob said in a whine. "Why can't I just watch? It's a virtual football game. Why treat it like such a big secret?"

"It's no secret. We just don't want you watching, that's all." Cal shrugged.

"Then I'll tune into every playing field round here until I find you," Jacob said. The threat was clear in his voice. "I've got a virtual play helmet too. You can't stop me watching you."

And with that, Jacob vanished from the screen.

Cal sighed and leaned back in his chair. He hadn't handled that very well, but Jacob got on his nerves. Cal turned to look at his virtual play helmet, which was hanging in the corner of his room. He shook his head. After every football game with Jenna and the rest, he grew to hate the helmet more and more.

Years and years ago, scientists had invented a way to play team games without contact with any other person. You sat in your own room, you connected up the virtual play helmet to your NC suit and you plugged it in. It didn't matter if the game was football, basketball, rounders or whatever – everyone else who was playing did the same. Then you decided where you were going to play, who was in your team and who was on the other side. Then everyone would link up and computers would do the rest.

It was virtual reality football.

Each player was in their room, all alone,
but it didn't look like that. It looked as if
you were on the field with everyone else – all
of you playing the game together. It was a
brilliant way to make sure that there was no
real contact between the players. Oh, you
could kick the ball and the NC suit made it
feel and look like you were kicking it. But
you weren't. It was all a computer game. It
wasn't real.

But real or not, you weren't allowed to tackle. A tackle, or even an attempt at a tackle, would get you sent off. Cal thought that it was the most stupid rule ever. Instead of tackles, you could only run so far with the ball before you had to pass, or the ball went to the other side. Those were the rules. No contact – even in virtual reality.

Cal sighed. He couldn't go back to playing by the rules, he just couldn't. Not after playing the way he and his friends played.

CHAPTER 4
FIXTURE

Later that morning, Cal called Jenna to decide what to do about the match.

"Are you alone?" he asked.

Jenna nodded. "Are we still on for this afternoon?"

"That depends," Cal said. "Has your brother given up yet?"

"What d'you think?" Jenna snorted.

Cal thought for a long moment. Should he call off the game? No, he wouldn't. He couldn't.

"We'll play, but we'll be very careful," he said. "Jacob's on your case, Jenna. You've got to be extra careful."

"Understood." Jenna nodded. And with that, she disconnected the call.

CHAPTER 5
KIT

That afternoon, Cal made his way out of the city to a deserted wasteland outside the gates. He asked himself over and over if he was doing the right thing.

He didn't have the answer.

Cal was the last to arrive. Everyone else was there before him. He looked around. Jacob wasn't there. Cal could feel every tense muscle in his body begin to relax.

"We thought you weren't going to show up," Jenna said.

"As if!" Cal grinned.

"Is it safe to play?" Andrew asked.

"Course it is," Cal said, and he began to take off his NC suit.

The others looked around before they did the same.

They always waited for Cal to take off his NC suit first. He and Andrew had been the first ones to play football without their suits. Then Tariq and Jenna had joined in – and then, over many months, their numbers had grown to ten true and trusted friends.

Cal kicked off his NC suit and stood in his shorts, NC boots and a T-shirt. The others did the same. Cal took a deep breath and raised his hands to the sky. The air dancing over his skin felt like a whisper from heaven. A slight breeze blew. It was amazing to think that, a year ago, Cal hadn't even known how good a breeze could feel as it sighed across his face.

CHAPTER 6
PITCH

Cal and the others stood in a circle, hand in hand. Cal marvelled at the feel of real fingers. Not virtual fingers or fingers enclosed in an NC glove but real live fingers! Clammy, sweaty, warm, soft, wonderful fingers! Even the best NC suit couldn't match that feeling of contact.

"Ready?" Cal asked everyone.

They all nodded.

"All for one and one for all and no one must know!" they all chanted. "Let's play!"

Tariq threw out the ball – it was a home-made one they'd made out of scrap plastic packed with soft wadding – and the game began.

Real tackles. Contact!

Real elbows. Contact!

And then Andrew scored a goal. Everyone gathered round him to pat him on the back or hug him or lift him into the air, even the players on the other side.

Cal beamed at everyone as they ran up and down the pitch. It was like being truly human for one afternoon a month. Only on this wasteland pitch did he feel alive. He loved its rough, broken surface – nothing like the perfect green grass of the virtual pitch. The result didn't matter. The game did. No screens, no computer programs, just real kids! Cal felt sure that flying and swooping and soaring couldn't be any better than the contact of real football.

But something was wrong.

One by one the players on the pitch froze and stared past Cal.

Cal's head snapped round to look too.

"So this is where you've all got to, is it?"

It was Jacob.

CHAPTER 7
KICK-OFF

No one spoke. No one moved. They all stared in horror. Jacob looked around and his eyes narrowed. Then he turned to Cal. His eyes fixed on Cal's shorts and boots and his T-shirt, which was damp with sweat.

"Jacob, you followed me!" Jenna shouted. "You toad! You shouldn't have …"

"No, Jenna. Leave it," Cal said.

"I told you I'd find you," Jacob said at last.

Silence.

"Physical contact of any kind is against the law," Jacob said. He tilted his head to one side, as if he was puzzled. "Aren't you afraid you're going to breathe in some germs or catch some disease from each other and die?"

"Well, it hasn't happened yet," Cal said. "So, no, we're not worried. And football is fun like this – contact football, real football. It's like nothing else on Earth. Do you want to try it?"

"You're only asking me so that I won't tell anyone what you're all up to," said Jacob.

"That's partly true," Cal said. "But you know about us now. Whether you tell or not is up to you, but don't go before you try it."

Jacob looked around again. Every eye was upon him.

"Even if I do play, I'll still tell on you," Jacob said.

Jenna opened her mouth to argue, but Cal got in first.

"That's up to you, Jacob," he said. His voice was calm, but he felt churned up with fear inside. "But you can't leave now, otherwise you'll always wonder what it would've been like. This is your chance to find out."

Everyone else moved up slowly to stand around Cal. They stood in a line and looked at Jacob. No one made any sudden movements. It was as if they didn't want to scare Jacob away.

CHAPTER 8
PLAYER

Jacob undid his gloves first and took them off. He stared down at his bare hands and clenched them. As he looked up, Cal smiled. Jacob's hands relaxed. He undid his NC suit and stepped out of it to stand in shorts and a T-shirt like everyone else.

"D'you want me to help you take off your helmet?" Cal said.

"No, I'll do it myself." Jacob's voice was low and nervous.

Jacob's fingers shook as he undid the straps at the sides of his helmet. He pulled it off his head with a gasp.

"You can be on my side," Cal said, and he
held out his hand. "OK?"

Jacob looked down at Cal's hand – and
worry and fear spread over his face. Cal
thrust his hand further forward.

"Take my hand! It won't bite you." He smiled.

After a pause, Jacob took hold of Cal's hand.

Cal recognised the shock and wonder on Jacob's face, because it had been on his face too the first time he shook hands at the start of a football match without his NC suit on. It had started off as a silly dare between two friends, but it had grown into something addictive. Cal's smile grew as Jacob looked at him with eyes wide with astonishment.

"Welcome to our game!" Cal grinned. Jacob was still holding his hand and he had to tug to pull it away. He turned to the others around him. "OK, team, Jacob's on our side," he said. "Let's give him hell!"

CHAPTER 9
TEAM

The next 45 minutes felt like one of the best times Cal had ever had – and it was some of the best football any of them had ever played as well. Players from both sides used any excuse to let Jacob have it! They bumped into him, tackled him – to the ground more often than not – brought him down, hacked him, elbowed him and even head-butted him in the stomach. That was his sister, Jenna.

And Jacob loved it!

He wasn't a bad player either. After his body had got used to running up and down the pitch, instead of playing a virtual game, it was as if he'd been part of the team for ever. He gave as good as he got, enjoying each knock he had with the others.

But all too soon, Cal had to call a halt. "Our time's up, guys," he said.

They stood on the pitch, panting and sweating.

"Could we play for just a little longer?" Andrew protested. Everyone nodded their agreement.

Cal shook his head. "You all know how this works. We're all meant to be round at someone else's house playing virtual football. If we're late home our parents will check up on us. We've got away with it so far – we don't want to blow it now."

Grumbling, as they did every month, the whole group formed a circle and held hands. Jacob stood and watched, not sure what was going on.

"Come on, Jacob – you too." Cal beckoned him over.

Jacob walked over to stand between Jenna
and Cal. He took hold of their hands, and he
became part of the circle.

"D'you know something?" Jenna smiled at
her brother. "You're not too bad!"

"That's the first time I can remember you smiling at me," Jacob told her.

"Are you still going to tell on us?" Cal asked.

The moment he spoke, the mood of the group changed. The circle was broken as hands dropped to sides. Some players looked down at their feet, some looked away at the city walls, a few looked at Cal. No one looked at Jacob.

"What do you think?" Jacob said at last.

"Jacob ..." Jenna didn't get any further.

She wasn't the only one who was disappointed. Cal felt his whole body slump with misery.

"How could I beat you all next time, if I told anyone?" Jacob said. "The secret's safe with me."

And Jacob started laughing. Moments later, everyone else was doing the same – at first in relief and then with real joy.

"You should've seen your faces." Jacob grinned, but then his smile faded. "I was going to tell – before I took my NC suit off, but it's different now. It feels as if we're all connected somehow."

"Welcome to our group," Cal said. "We have an oath we say before and after each game. If you're going to be part of us, you must say it too – but before that, PILE ON! Get him, everyone, for winding us up!"

And half of them piled on top of Jacob before the other half lifted him high on their shoulders.

"He doesn't even look like my brother any more," Jenna whispered to Cal. "He looks different somehow."

"Yeah. For the first time he looks real, part of a team like the rest of us," said Cal. "I think we've reached him. I think we've made contact."

Our books are tested
for children and young people by
children and young people.

Thanks to everyone who consulted on
a manuscript for their time and effort in
helping us to make our books better
for our readers.

Also by *Malorie Blackman* ...

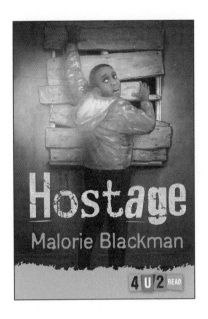

"I'll make sure your dad never sees you again!"

Blindfolded. Alone.

Angela has no idea where she is or what will happen next. The only thing she knows is that she's been kidnapped. Is she brave enough to escape?

More **4u2read** titles ...

I Never Liked Wednesdays
ROGER MCGOUGH

It was a Wednesday if I remember rightly. I never liked Wednesdays for some reason. I could never spell 'Wednesday' for a start. And it always seemed to rain on Wednesdays. And there were two days to go before the weekend ...

Wartman
MICHAEL MORPURGO

Dilly's life was great till he got a wart on his knee.

Now everyone stares and calls him 'Wartman'.

How can Dilly get rid of the wart and get his life back on track?

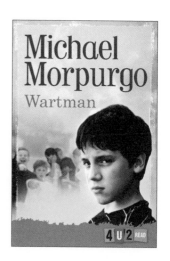

4U2 READ

Nadine Dreams of Home

BERNARD ASHLEY

Nadine finds Britain real scary. Not scary like soldiers, or burning buildings, or the sound of guns. But scary in other ways. If only her father were here with them, but they have no idea if they will ever see her father again. But then Nadine finds a special picture, and dreams a special dream ...

All Sorts to Make a World

JOHN AGARD

Shona's day has been packed with characters. First there was 3.2-million-year-old Lucy in the Natural History Museum, and then Pinstripe Man, Kindle Woman, Doctor Bananas and the iPod Twins. Now Shona and her dad are on a Tube train that's stuck in a tunnel and everyone around them is going ... bananas!

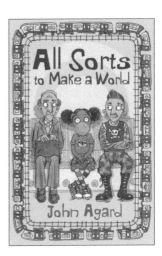

www.barringtonstoke.co.uk